Everything Big Starts Somewhere Small

The Story of the Caleb White Project

Enjoy!

Tammi Landry-Gilder

By Tammi Landry-Gilder

Illustrated By Diego Farah, Isabella Farah, and Sofia Farah

ISBN: 978-0-692-96632-7

For Caleb - Always follow your dreams.
For Melissa - Always remember what you've accomplished.
For Noah - Always be yourself because your self is a pretty awesome dude.

Text and illustrations copyright © 2017 by Tammi Landry-Gilder. All rights reserved. Published by TLG Press, LLC, 7249 S. Oak Ct. W., West Bloomfield, MI 48323.

Printed in the United States of America

The images in this book were designed and drawn by three talented teens, Diego Farah, Isabella Farah, and Sofia Farah, who are committed to volunteering, youth service, fundraising for needy families, and fighting for animal rights. To view their work, please visit www.kharts.org.

On a cold day in December, Caleb and his parents drove to Detroit to see the circus. The large, gray elephants and colorful, crazy clowns fascinated him. He especially liked the acrobats and tightrope walkers. He filled his little tummy with popcorn and ice cream, and drank pop, which his mom usually never let him have.

"I think this is my best day ever!" Caleb hugged his dad as he watched the tigers stand on their tiny stools in the middle of the biggest circus ring.

After the amazing circus show, Caleb and his parents walked back toward the parking garage to find their car.

"I loved that circus! Dad, did you see that clown with the huge, pink hair? He was the funniest of them all." Caleb yawned and rubbed his eyes.

"Someone is tired." Caleb's dad winked at him.

"I'm not tired!" Caleb frowned and yawned again. He thought about his warm, cozy bed at home and his very favorite stuffed toy, Paws the Puppy, who was just right for snuggling.

The winter wind whipped across Caleb's face as he pulled up the collar of his warm winter coat. His mom opened her purse and pulled out Caleb's red winter hat and gloves.

"Thanks, Mom." Caleb put his gloves on as his mom pushed his hat way down on his head so that it covered his pink ears.

"I'm freezing!"
Caleb held his mom's hand and skipped toward the parking garage.

As Caleb and his parents rounded a corner, Caleb noticed a pile of muddied, stained clothes, lumped up against a building. As they got closer to the building, he realized it wasn't a pile of dirty clothes on the ground. That pile was a person!

A man slept right there on the sidewalk. His white beard reminded Caleb of Santa Claus.

"Mom," Caleb whispered, "Why is that man sleeping on the sidewalk? It's so cold out here. Why doesn't he just go home?"
Caleb's mom held his hand, and looked down at the sleeping man.

"Well, that man doesn't have a home. He's homeless, so he sometimes has to sleep outside."

Caleb stopped walking. "He doesn't have a house?"

"Not everyone can afford a house. Sometimes if people lose their jobs or have a hard time in life, they can become homeless. Some people can't even afford food." Caleb's mom adjusted the hat on Caleb's head so that it covered his ears.

Caleb remembered the yummy food he ate at the circus. "Mom, can we go back to the circus and buy him some popcorn?" Caleb tugged on his mom's hand.

Caleb's mom opened her purse again, took out a five dollar bill, and left it in a red, plastic cup sitting next to the sleeping man.

"Do you see those coins in his cup? He probably uses that money to buy food." Caleb's mom put her arm around Caleb's shoulder. "Maybe he can buy a sandwich with the money you gave him." Caleb smiled.

Caleb still didn't understand how someone could live without money. He knew that sometimes his mom and dad couldn't always afford to buy him the most expensive toys, but he had a house. It was a small house, and it wasn't fancy, but it was warm and filled with all of their comfortable and favorite things, like blankets and pillows, and toys and pictures.

"How does the man remember his family without a house full of pictures? How does he eat without a refrigerator full of food? Where does he take a shower?" Caleb was worried. He didn't want this man, or any person, sleeping outside in the cold. It wasn't right. It wasn't fair.

"Dad, we need to buy that man a house," Caleb said as he got into the car.

"Oh gosh, we can't afford to buy him a house, but there is something we can do," said Caleb's dad as he drove down the street. "We can make a donation to a homeless shelter. How about that?"

"Yes!" Caleb was excited. "What's a homeless shelter?"

Caleb's mother explained that a shelter is a place where homeless people can go for a warm bed, daily meals, or medical assistance. "Sometimes people can live there until they find a job and a home of their own."

Caleb wrinkled his forehead.
"I think we could do more than donate to a homeless shelter. We could visit and make friends there. We could take clothes and food, too. Can children be homeless, Mom?"

"Yes. Sometimes whole families are homeless." Caleb's mom looked sad, and Caleb's eyes filled with tears. He couldn't imagine kids his own age who didn't live in a happy, comfortable home with their families.

Caleb remembered how hard his parents had worked to save up enough money to take him to the circus.

I bet homeless kids never go to the circus. Caleb started to cry. Right then, Caleb decided he had a lot more work to do in life. Too many people in the world needed his help.

For the next few days, Caleb and his mom researched ways to start an organization to help the homeless.

"I hope I can figure all of this out." Caleb's mom tapped her finger nervously as she stared at the computer screen.

"Of course you can, Mom. You are the smartest person I know.".

Caleb White Project

"The kind of organization we need is called a non-profit. We can raise money or collect clothing and supplies to give to the homeless. We need to fill out special paperwork so we can get to work and start helping people." Caleb's mom explained. Caleb beamed. He felt good knowing he would soon be helping others who were just like the Santa Claus man he'd seen sleeping outside that day after the circus show.

"But Mom, what will we call our organization?" Caleb asked. "Well, since this was all your idea, we should call it the Caleb White Project. What do you think?"

Caleb smiled. "I like it."

Soon, the Caleb White Project was officially born and Caleb made his plans for helping as many people in need as he could.

"The first thing we can do is make up some bags or boxes for homeless people. We will add food and water to each bag, along with a blanket, soap, and other things people need," Caleb told his mom. "Then we can go to Detroit and hand out the bags to every single homeless person we see."

"I like that idea, Caleb!" Caleb's mom gave him a big hug.

Caleb called all of his family members and friends asking for donations to fill the bags for the homeless people. Caleb and his mom visited local businesses asking for donations, too.
Very soon, The Caleb White Project had twenty filled bags to give to those in need.

"This is awesome!" Caleb jumped up and pumped his fist into the air.

On a very cold Saturday morning, Caleb and his mom drove to Detroit, not far from the big building where they'd seen the circus, and close to where Caleb spotted the homeless Santa Claus man.

They handed out every bag they had to anyone they saw who lived on the streets. They met Cyril, a man who used to build cars for one of the big three auto companies. They met Lucy, who hadn't seen her children in 14 years. Caleb introduced himself to Stan who lost both of his legs in the Vietnam War.

"Caleb, thank you so much for these wonderful bags filled with so many things I need. This will help me so much!" Lucy gave Caleb a big, warm hug.

"My, my my... I don't think I've ever met such nice young man. These thick socks in here will keep my feet warm all winter long." Cyril dug through all the items in his bag, then he gave Caleb a hug.

"I think I got more hugs today than I've ever had in my whole life!" Caleb exclaimed as his mom started the car to head back home. "Can you believe how nice everyone was, Mom? And did you see how thankful they all were? I think we made a difference today." Caleb shivered as he watched the snowflakes land on the windshield.
"I'm really glad we put blankets in those bags." Caleb yawned.

As Caleb drifted off to sleep on the drive home, he dreamed of giving children in need toys and books and clothes. He dreamed of serving dinner to people living in homeless shelters. He dreamed of visiting and playing games with Cyril, Lucy, and the Santa Claus man. When he woke up, he made all his dreams come true.

The End

The Caleb White Project (CWP), started in 2011, now has more than six major programs that directly help the homeless in Detroit and surrounding areas. With a Board of Directors comprised of ten intelligent, outgoing, giving, and talented teens, CWP continues to educate the public about homelessness, fight poverty, encourage youth volunteerism and leadership, and make the world a better place.

After all, "Everything big starts somewhere small." - Caleb White

Caleb White Project Board Members

Caleb White - Caleb attends Detroit Catholic Central High School where he wrestles and runs cross country and track. He served as the President of the National Junior Honor Society in eighth grade at Clifford H. Smart Middle School. Caleb was named America's Top Youth Volunteer in 2015, and has also received the President's Volunteer Service Award, the Governor's Youth Leader of the Year Award, and the Kohl's Cares Scholarship. He serves on the Youth Council for the Detroit Rescue Mission and the Youth Advisory Board for Purposeful Networks. He plays the french horn, piano, and drums. Caleb carries a 4.3 GPA and hopes to one day attend either the University of Notre Dame or the University of Michigan.

Colin Stewart - Colin is a junior at Detroit Catholic Central High School. He is a member of the Academic Team, chess club, French club, and HOSA club. Colin has a 5.0 GPA, the highest in his class, and has been the recipient of the President's Award for outstanding grades. He hopes to attend the University of Michigan or MIT to study biomedical engineering. Colin enjoys volunteering, playing golf, and skiing in his spare time.

Grant Landry - Grant attends Cranbrook Kingswood Preparatory School in Bloomfield Hills, Michigan, where he is on the Dean's List, carrying a 4.0 GPA, and plays basketball. As a member of the National Junior Honor Society at Clifford H. Smart Middle School, Grant successfully chaired the largest community service project in the history of the school's Honor Society. Grant is a First Degree Black Belt in Taekwondo, and has been chosen to participate in Northwestern University's NUMATS program for Gifted and Talented Students. Grant plays second base for the Lakes Area Baseball Association, enjoys traveling, and playing video games in his spare time.

Brendin Yatooma - Brendin attends Detroit Catholic Central High School where he is a member of both the varsity football and wrestling teams. He is passionate about helping the homeless and enjoys spending time with Veterans and their families, thanking them for their service. Brendin has a 4.1 GPA and plans to study sports medicine in college.

Katy LeWalk - Katy is a senior at Divine Child High School in Dearborn, Michigan, where she holds a 4.07 GPA, is a varsity basketball player, and captain of the track team. She is President of the Divine Child Varsity Club, which promotes service and leadership among those in the highest level of high school athletics, and Executive Board Member of the National Honor Society, and is a Eucharistic Minister at her church and school. Katy hopes to attend the United States Naval Academy or the United States Military Academy at West Point in the future.

Joey Gusumano - Joey is a sophomore at Orchard Lake St. Mary's where he is an honor roll student. He was drawn to the Caleb White Project because he has a passion for helping others. Joey enjoys playing lacrosse, golf, and video games. He hopes to attend Marquette University in Milwaukee and play lacrosse for the Golden Eagles. He would like to pursue a career in sports medicine, and one day coach younger children in a variety of sports. His most important goal in life is to "make the world a better place."

Ben Kamali - Ben attends Detroit Catholic Central High School where he is a member of the wrestling team, winning the 2016 State Championship at 103 pounds. He is currently ranked 14th in the country at 113 pounds and has verbally committed to Iowa State University where he will wrestle and study Kinesiology. Ben is very passionate at giving back to the community and wants to make a positive change in the world.

Abby Brien - Abby is a junior at Northville High School where she is a member of the National Honor Society. She was first introduced to the Caleb White Project by attending a Game Night at the shelter event. Abby has always had a love for helping others and found the CWP to be the perfect fit. When she isn't volunteering, she enjoys playing volleyball and spending time with her family and friends. Abby and her family are huge college football fans! After graduation, she hopes to fulfill her dream of attending Medical School at the University of Michigan.

You, too, can make a difference!

Log Your Volunteer Work Hours Here

Organization	Date	Number of Hours

You, too, can make a difference!

Log Your Volunteer Work Hours Here

Organization	Date	Number of Hours